T0209182

Hello,
My
Name is
Heidi...

Books by Randy J. Hartman

Romance 101 for men, Recipes for the game of love
ISBN: 0-595-13128-ZX

The Key to Hypnosis
ISBN: 0-595-13956-6

Trance Scripts
ISBN: 0-595-14070-X

Hypnotic Work in Progress
ISBN: 0-595-14188-9

Raising Randy
ISBN: 978-14401-2565-2

Tell Me a Joke, Please
ISBN: 978-4401-2145-8

Hello, My Name is Heidi...

Randy J. Hartman

iUniverse

HELLO, MY NAME IS HEIDI...

iUniverse books may be ordered through booksellers or by contacting:

iUniverse
1663 Liberty Drive
Bloomington, IN 47403
www.iuniverse.com
844-349-9409

ISBN: 978-1-6632-5579-2 (sc)
ISBN: 978-1-6632-5578-5 (e)

Library of Congress Control Number: 2023916287

Print information available on the last page.

iUniverse rev. date: 08/25/2023

Contents

Introduction

<u>Hello, My Name is Heidi</u> is a book that offers up some tongue-in-cheek insight into what a boxer puppy had to go through to train her human companion. This provides some very entertaining insight into a dog's life as seen through the eyes of a boxer puppy.

Move over Garfield, Heidi is the new kid on the block. She is quite demanding at times with her human companion, Randy. Heidi has made it a labor of love to train Randy to anticipate her every need, and her needs are many. More often than not life in their household became a war of willpowers.

All of the incidents in this book are real; it's really how one perceives the situation as to whether it becomes humorous. It has been said that beauty is in the eyes of the beholder, and humor is also in the eyes of the beholder. It's important to try and put a humorous frame around the events in our lives to make life more bearable for us.

If you have ever wondered what is going on in your dog's mind, this book should offer you some tongue-in-cheek answers to this question. It has been reported that most dogs mature to the same approximate level as a three-year-old child. This gives you an idea of what you are up against in raising dogs, as well as children. By age three children are talking and dogs are not, but don't write them off yet. Dogs have developed their ways of communicating their needs, wants and feelings.

Heidi is a good example of how dogs can develop an advanced form of communication. We have this human delusion that we train our dogs to respond to our commands. Or, are we trained by our dogs to reward them for their good behavior? Some days it feels like a fine line between who is trained and who is really the trainer.

Chapter One

Heidi Who?

As I try to remember back in time, ooh, that hurts my brain! My earliest memories seem to be to a place close to my mom. I had three brothers and four sisters that made my life miserable. I was the baby of the family who lived on a smelly blanket with eight dogs pooping on it. Don't even try to imagine that bad smell.

Trying to eat was a nightmare; I usually had to kick some serious boxer butt to get one of my mother's teats. My mom was mellow most of the time, at least until we started growing teeth! Then there was my dad; he was the strong silent type. Usually he just stood back and watched us with that goofy smile on his face as if to say, "Look what I did". He sure did it right - A litter of eight pups! That's enough to make any stud boxer smile. My mom and dad had some fancy names that were long and hard to pronounce. Randy gave me the registered name of Heidi Susan Hartman. We'll have to talk later about how I got the middle name of Susan. Now I'm sure everyone will

1

think because of my name that I'm some kind of human but no, I'm a very proud female boxer that is tan with white flashing (markings) on all four feet with a white chest. I've got great big black lips, and my lower teeth stick out when I smile. Randy sometimes calls me his vampire boxer! I also have one black toenail on each paw. I pride myself on driving the boy boxers crazy! Girlfriend, I got it going on for me. The rascals are always trying to kiss me by licking my big old sweet lips.

Randy picked me up right from the litter and brought me to my new home. He said that I was the *runt* of the litter. I don't know what that means, but I think I resent it. Life at my new home was sure different without my brothers and sisters around. I was the only animal in the house, except for Randy. That guy is a story all by himself.

I was a little scared and lonely the first night in m new home without my pack. I started crying and whining in my kennel until Randy gave up and put me on the bed with him. Then I slept like a big dog. That went on for about two weeks before Randy forced me back into my kennel at night. Well, that sure didn't work very well. Now two years later Randy still has to take me by the collar and lead me the kennel, as I refuse to surrender to the dreaded kennel prison. My rightful place is with my pack leader on the bed, I finally convinced him of that fact. My hard headedness is one of my many endearing traits.

Just newly weaned from my mother I was fed moist canned dog food. Yummy! Now Randy is mixing my wet dog food with dry dog food, Yuk, I don't know if I'll ever get used to this stuff. Whatever Randy is eating smells better than my dog food, but he doesn't want to share with me. How rude! I would be glad to share my food with him. Over time I discovered that dry dog food seems to be an acquired taste. Around the kitchen and dining room table I'm the resident vacuum on four-legs. If it hits the floor, its mine baby, don't touch it.

Potty training was the worst ten months of my life. Yes, I did say ten months. Remember my endearing trait of being hard-headed? Every time I would pee or drop a dog log Randy would get upset with me and make me go outside. I don't know what he thought I would do out there, as I already did my business in the house. For Pete's sake, I don't know what it takes to get him trained! So to avoid Randy getting upset, I would sneak around where he couldn't see me and drop a log, but the odor would usually give me away. By the time Randy found the evidence I would just look innocent and pretend I didn't know who that poop belonged to, maybe just a phantom dog passing through the house? So the potty saga continues. By the time I stopped piddling in the house I had pretty much destroyed the carpet in the guest room. The urine had soaked through the carpet and into the wooden floor.

Randy had a guy come in and tear out the carpet and put a clear coat of sealant down to stop the urine odor before having a new carpet installed.

A huge revelation came to me in my first month in my new home, as if a gift from the great dog spirit in the sky. I discovered this thing called a *cookie*. I was so wonderfully surprised to find out that there are many different *cookies*. Unfortunately the humans have to dispense the cookies because they have the opposable thumb to open the packages and treat jars. My treat jar with cookies sits on the kitchen counter and Randy hides his cookies in the cupboard. So we dogs usually have to humble ourselves and humor our human companions by doing silly things so we can get the very tasty cookies that we dogs revere.

I try not to spoil Randy too much, because then he would expect it all the time. At night I let Randy sleep in the big bed with me. We are both happier that way. Once Randy settles down for the night I go to the foot of the bed and curl up by his feet, just barely touching his legs. I can't seem to shake the old pack mentality. Some nights I just can't get a decent amount of sleep because the big guy is tossing and turning. I can remember one morning waking up and my head was lying on his arm and my face was looking at his face. What a rude sight to wake up to in the morning!

One area I excel at is Guard Duty. When the doorbell rings I put on my big girl bark and try to sound mean. I'm not dumb enough to run to the door to see who it is; that's what I've got Randy for. He tells me that I'm such a good girl for sounding the alarm. He's especially proud of me when I stand on my back legs and bark; it makes me look like a giant boxer!

I've had to teach Randy the hard way not to ignore me when I want to play. A couple of months ago he made the mistake of lying down for a nap about the same time I wanted to play. I took the big guy a toy to play with me, but he rolled over and went to sleep. I was more than a little disturbed with Randy, so I was going to teach him a lesson to not ignore his princess at playtime. While he slept, I took his right shoe from his bedroom and hid it from him. Behind the recliner was not a good spot, or not the laundry either, so I put his shoe under the bed in the guest room. I was lying in the living room having a leisurely chew on my rope toy when I heard Randy call my name. Well, I wasn't in the mood to see him yet, but he came looking for me anyway. He asked where his other shoe was, as if I was really going to tell him! Fortunately for Randy that Kathy stopped by and helped him find his shoe. I hope the big guy learned his lesson now to not ignore this girl's need to play.

Humans do take a lot of work to train properly. Randy is such a space cadet and at times he almost forgets that

I'm here, and that isn't going to happen! I've worked out a signal for Randy so he can remember to give me a treat, I call it a treat on command.

If Randy is ignoring me, I'll run around behind him and stand on my hind legs and push on his butt with my front paws, sort of like pushing the secret button on the cookie dispenser! You would be amazed how well that seems to work most of the time. Other times it just ticks him off.

Randy does an okay job of trying to spoil me. He bought me a dog bed that looks like a miniature couch, burgundy with gold piping. It fits perfectly under a wall table. I usually don't clock much sleep time on my couch; usually I'll just lie there and chew on a toy and try to look cute. I also have a three-foot floor pillow to lounge on. We keep that on the bedroom floor and it's usually unused. My personal favorite bed is the one Randy put in the truck for me. He found a nice oblong fur dog bed that he puts on the passenger's seat. I feel so regal riding in the truck. The fur bed is my throne and a cookie is my scepter as I hold court in the kingdom before me. Usually I will sit upright in the passenger's seat with my left paw on the center console as I survey my domain while Randy drives the big red chariot down the road.

One of my favorite places to go bye-bye to is the Top Dog Canine Daycare in Olympia, Washington. When Randy says we are going to daycare I get happy in a hurry. So many dogs to play with and so little time to play in eight hours. When we pull up in front of the daycare the dogs bark at me to hurry on in to play. The humans there take such good care of us dogs. At mid-day we take a time-out and have a cookie with some quiet time. That's usually enough to recharge my batteries and I'm ready to play again. At daycare they call me Miss Wiggles, as I wag my entire body when I'm happy. Randy usually brings me to daycare at least once a week to play hard and socialize with all the other dogs there.

Our other special place to go is the local Dairy Queen. I get so excited when Randy pulls into the drive through at Dairy Queen; I can't sit still and sometimes I lose control and start drooling. Usually Randy orders me a medium size dish of vanilla ice cream, no spoon please. In the back seat of the truck Randy has an aluminum dog dish that he dumps my ice cream into. What a fantastic treat! I'm glad I'm not lactose intolerant. Normally Randy will park in the shade while I eat my ice cream and he can enjoy his cherry slushy. I've been begging him for a hot dog with ketchup, but no luck. I guess he's afraid he might spoil me.

A year after having the guest room carpet installed, we had another carpet incident happen. It was one of my crazy moments at about three in the morning. Randy was asleep and I was pacing around the living room on burglar patrol like I usually do, when an ink pen caught my attention. It was a shiny gold ink pen that Randy keeps on the table beside the love seat where he sits in the evening. I crawled up there to sniff it and discovered it smelt like a cookie. Well, you know where this story is going. The smell of the ink pen was so alluring, just like a drug known as a cookie. I took the pen to the middle of the carpeted floor and started chewing on it, thinking that Randy must be hiding a cookie inside. Oops, no cookie was found there, but I discovered about a four-inch black ink stain on the gray/white carpet that leaked out from the ink pen.

You are right, Randy was hopping mad at me. He chewed me out, up one side and down the other. It's good he doesn't stay mad very long, he told me he always wanted new carpet in the living room. I did spend the rest of the day on best boxer behavior. That was hard to do since I'm a highly devoted playgirl, but under the circumstances I kept it low key all day.

Randy does come with his baggage; he has two sons and their families. Terry is the oldest son that lives in Olympia with his family. I really have not come to trust Terry yet. He talks loudly and mean so I keep my distance from him. His son Mykel has become my favorite play friend. He knows how to really mix it up when it comes to playing. We play hard and long, and I really enjoy the playtime we have. Now that Mykel is getting older his attention is turning to girls and cars a lot, so I just wait for any opportunity to play.

Chapter Two

Hunk of Burning Love

Even boxer girls need some love in their lives. I have two boxer guys that make my little heart go pitter-patter. One male boxer is just not enough; you know what I mean girlfriend? These two guys are brothers, so I have to play it carefully. You know how guys talk about the girls. I just love a walk on the wild side of life.

The first boy boxer is named Jaeger and he lives with his mom in Lacey, Washington. His whole name is German, "Jaeger Meister". In English it means *Master Hunter*. Many people seem to think it's only the name of a German liqueur. Randy had known Jaeger for about four years before I came along. Randy told me that Jaeger was a good guy with real good manners. Randy was foolish enough to tell me that I should take notes on how good Jaeger behaves when we visit him. Like that is really going to happen, not.

Jaeger has large brown eyes that look like two pools of dark chocolate that burn a hole right through me, the cutest floppy ears, a fawn-colored coat with white markings, and on his feet white markings look like little white ankle socks. With the faint odor of Nutro dog food on his breath, it's enough to take my breath away and make my heart skip a beat!

What a stud-muffin he is! He strikes such a handsome pose in the yard when he lifts his leg to pee, truly a breath-taking remarkable sight. I have no problem with this handsome gentleman smelling my behind; take a long whiff of this package my dear. While this handsome hunk is a real turn-on, he does not have much stamina in the playing department. I try to go slow, so I do not wear this old guy out too quickly with too much running and boxer dancing.

You say you have not heard of *boxer dancing*? That is what Randy calls it when I stand on my two hind legs and spar/box with another boxer. It looks serious, but it's all play. I may be smaller that Jaeger, but I'm wiry and full of energy. Sometimes my nickname is the *energizer boxer*, as I just keep going and going.

Jaeger has a brother named *Yoshi* who lives in Seattle with Bill and Rhonda and enjoying the urban lifestyle. I often refer to him as my *yuppie puppy*. Yoshi is white with a very pretty pink skin showing through. His whole body is white except for a tan circle around one eye! Maybe in a previous life he was a pirate boxer on the high seas. Yoshi is the same age as Jaeger but has more stamina to play. That old boy can usually put me through quite a workout. Yoshi is not as much of a gentleman as Jaeger, but sometimes I like it rough! He is a lot of fun and a ball of energy, although he does have a sensitive stomach that keeps him thin and wiry looking. Despite that, he does cut a fine figure on the lawn.

There is a lot of playing and romance going on with my guys, but we all have been *fixed* so nothing sexy is going on, except for getting my behind sniffed a lot. It's just as well this way; I would not want to put up with seven or eight little puppies that were always hungry and making potty.

Sometimes Randy and I meet up with Jaeger and his mom at the Fort Steilacoom Off-Leash Dog Park where there is a monthly meet-up of all sizes, shapes, and colors of boxers. Some of those boxers are fun and some boxers surprise me when they could run faster than me. Just briefly after leaving the dog park Kathy and Randy left Jaeger and I in the car while they had lunch. What a special day it was, after we got home, I dictated a letter to Randy to send to Jaeger and his mom. The letter read:

Dear Jaeger and Kathy,

I wanted to thank you for a wonderful day of playing and adventure, and for feeding Randy lunch, as he gets grouchy if he is hungry.

Jaeger my dear, thank you for a wonderful run in the park. It was fun to stretch my legs and giggle as we ran through the mud puddles – you are such a wild heartbreaker at times.

I hope you did not tell your mom what we did in the backseat while they were gone shopping? I still remember your slobber in my jowls with a hint of Nutro in the air. Remember now that a gentleman dog never kisses and tells...

Until we get a chance to sniff again.

Forever yours my hunk of burning love,
Heidi

Even we four-legged females desire a little romance when the excellent opportunity arises. Jaeger is the romantic while Yoshi has the *bad-boy boxer image,* the strong forward brute that just has way with the girls, then runs off looking for a cookie. I feel like I have the best of both worlds going for me with these two guys vying for my attention. Since they are brothers I must be sly so I do not start a sibling rivalry between them.

Jaeger, what a silly boy. He and I were spending the day at *Top Dog Canine Daycare* in Olympia just playing hard and meeting other dogs. That afternoon I had a *paw-acure*, that is what you humans call a pedicure. The lady that snipped my toenails accidently made one nail bleed a little, so they put me in a kennel for five minutes to get the bleeding to stop, and poor Jaeger was so upset he kept pacing the floor by my kennel until I was released. That big lug nut was so worried about me; it did make me feel special.

Okay Randy let's put a plug in it already. It's hard to believe at times that one human being can produce such fowl smells! Randy has said several times over that he's lactose intolerant, but I still it's near impossible for any human being to produce such. He is more foul smelling then a German Shephard. The other day a Doberman Pincher walked past us and started gagging and nearly passed out as Randy was leaking gas! I couldn't help snickering when that happened. I could go on for hours talking about Randy's gas. But a more interesting tale that definite and peculiar realm of Boxer dog gas. A phenomenon that is both hilarious and pungent. I'll share with you the misadventures of Heidi and her notorious gas escapades.

Heidi is also the proud owner of a powerful gas factory that resides in her belly. Her digestive system possesses the uncanny ability to produce gas that could rival even the most potent of skunks. I was feeling good, wagging my stubby tail. So I decided to share my gas prowess with Randy and his family as they gathered around the dinner table. There was a wonderful aroma of a delectable meal wafting through the air. My belly was just churning with anticipation.

Unknown to everyone Heidi had been preparing for this moment. With a sly grin she unleashed her creation, and the room was instantly engulfed in a noxious cloud of Boxer gas! All the humans coughed, their eyes watering, desperately gasping for fresh air. Meanwhile I sat there proudly wagging my tail as if I had just won a prestigious gas competition!

Oh Heidi, what on earth did you eat? The laughter started between gasps of clean air. There I sit, feigned innocent, my eyes wide and innocent, as if to say" who, me. It must be some cosmic twist of fate!" But deep down I knew the truth. My Boxer gas was my secret superpower. A weapon of mass hilarity that could be deployed at will. This was the beginning of my legacy as the "notorious Gas Master."

From that day forward, no room in the house was safe from my potent emissions. Whether it was the cozy living room, a ride with the windows rolled up, or during the most inopportune moments like family gathering or important meetings. I had developed a knack for making a grand entrance. Randy would often say, "Heidi, how can something as fowl come from someone as cute as you."

But despite the occasional smelly mishaps, Heidi knew she was loved. Her gas became a source of endless jokes and unforgettable memories. A reminder that even in the most unexpected moments, laughter could still triumph. The legend of Heidi the Boxer and her horrendous gas lives on. Her gas would tear of laughter, uncontrollable giggles and perhaps a few open windows. Amidst it all Heidi's charming personality and her ability to bring joy to even the smelliest situation made her an unforgettable and beloved member of the family.

So, the next time you encounter a Boxer dog with a mischievous glint in her eyes, beware for you might find yourself at the mercy of a formidable gas factory. A force that can turn any into a laughter filled gas chamber. Remember during the smelliest moments, a good sense of humor can be the best air freshener. With that said, Heidi the Boxer proudly wags her tale, her gas emitting legacy etched into the annals of doggy history.

Chapter Three

Have crate, will travel!

Randy said it's time to "saddle up" and load up in the truck for a bye-bye. I don't care where we are going if I get to ride! I just love it when we are driving down the road and I can stick my head out the truck window and take in all those wonderful smells as the air makes my ears flutter in the breeze. It is difficult for me to get my nose out the window with this on called a seatbelt thingy. I don't understand why I would have to wear a seatbelt harness thingy when I see other dogs riding without them on and able to fully enjoy all the smells outside. It's almost a curse to be able to smell so much.

I think Randy did say something about a grooming appointment for me. I have no idea what that means, but I sure hope it taste good! We've pulled up in front of a building with big red letters on it. I can't remember ever being here before. Should be a good place as I have seen three dogs walk in there with their owners.

Oh crap, I don't like the sounds of what I heard Randy saying something about a bath and paint my toenails pink! What the hell is Randy trying to do to me? Once before Randy tried to give me a bath, but that bombed out. I think Randy got the worse end of the bath. I don't even like to go outside when it's raining, let alone standing still while someone is trying to hose me down with soap and water.

The girl giving me this bath is bigger than I am, so I guess I don't have much choice but to bite my lips and get it done. I was determined to not let this bath stuff happen without making sure everyone know I'm pissed. Once that bath was done, I certainly got a rude surprise. Not only did I get my toenail trimmed, I got my first ever, and last, nail polish applied to my toenails in a soft pink color. Hello there, someone tell Randy that I'm a dog, not a female human! I think I lost all my doggie dignity that day. I spent the next three days slowly chewing that damn polish my toenails.

We stopped and seen Kathy and my Boxer buddy Jaeger to show off my toenail polish job. Kathy said it was quite pretty. Jaeger on the other hand started laughing hilariously. He licked my toenails and let me know that he was glad that boy Boxers didn't wear nail polish. I really started to double down on my effort to chew that nail polish off. Jaeger, I want you to know for the time being that you are on my shit list!

All the humans we saw over the next few days thought that the polish was pretty, while all the other dogs in the neighborhood just snicked when I would walk by them.

Jaeger had come to stay with us for a few days while Kathy was out of town. I got even Jaeger by telling him that if he heard water running in the bathroom he had best run and hide because he was going to get a bath and his toenail painted a right red color! That toenail painting thingy craze did continue twice before Randy finally gave up on it.

On the other side of my fence lived a pair of big mouth Doberman Pinchers. Fred and Mable were their names. Fred, well he was the strong silent type while Mabel wouldn't hardly shut up once she was outside. She would run her big mouth constantly; you know what I mean girlfriend? When she was outside, I would usually slip back through my dog door into the living room. There would be Mable, still going on by herself and nagging on Fred. The only way she would shut up was when her humans would bring her back inside. By contrast, Fred would hangout quietly in his backyard sniffing and making sure he peed on everything so he could mark it for himself. Fred and Jaeger had some shared traits, mainly the macho strong silent type.

A road trip, I wasn't sure what that meant. Randy and Kathy were planning a road trip through Idaho, Montana,

Wyoming and Colorado. Once we loaded up and got underway, I was delighted to find out that this road trip was a real long opportunity to go bye-bye! Jaeger and I had the backseat of the car all to ourselves. The first day we traveled from Olympia, Washington to a motel in Montana where we spent the night. After a full day of riding and having an adventure, it was good to get a good night of sleep.

The following day we continued east in Montana to a place called "Custer's Last Stand". Kathy and Randy took a tour of the place, but all I seen was rolling prairies for miles.

Jaeger and I were happy for any opportunity to take a pee break and stretch our legs and get some much-needed sniffing time. For miles and miles in any direction there was only rolling prairies, tumbleweeds and Antelope everywhere. To help pass the time Jaeger would try to tell me jokes, usually that kind of "Dad jokes" I heard the humans talk about. My favorite joke went like this.

A Doberman, Labrador Retriever and a Boxer cross the rainbow bridge at the same time and end up standing before God. God ask them what they believe in. The Doberman said, "I believe in discipline, training and loyalty to my owner", God said good for you, you can sit on my right side. The Labrador said, "I believe in love and affection for my master and world peace." "Wow", said God, you may take a seat on my left. Then God turned to the Boxer and asked, "What do you believe in?" The Boxer looks at God and says, I believe you're sitting in my seat!

On our drive back to Washington we spent one night at a motel in the middle of the red desert in Wyoming called "Little America". It was there that Jaeger, and I got an unexpected experience. Right after supper Randy took us outside so Jaeger and I could relieve ourselves after a robust dinner of Nutro. We found a few trees among what seemed to be a sea of tumbleweeds and started walking towards the trees when to our surprise we seen a strange animal pop out from under the tree. It was a huge jackrabbit that seen us coming. Jaeger was so startled that he stood up on his back legs. I thought that poor Jaeger was going to have a stroke! The jackrabbit ran into the sage brush and disappeared. Hell, no girlfriend, I wasn't going to chase after that creature. Jaeger was trying his best to protect me from, but I could see he was really upset at this turn of events.

Randy was okay with most of the neighbors, with one exception. The dingbat woman that lived directly behind us. She seemed to be a real hysterical nut job! Her and her boyfriend were growing pot in their garage. You might ask, just how crazy was the neighbor woman, On one occasion she came over and knocked on my door and told Randy that his lawn sprinkler was getting her gravel and beauty bark wet, and he needed to stop doing that as she was having a party at her house on her patio later in the day, and that in the future stop getting her back yard wet. What a nut job.

Our neighborhood had more than its fair share of strange people living there. Most of the dogs in the hood were little nippers, beware of the ankle biters! One of the rudest dogs in the neighborhood was an un-cut German Shepard named Bruno. It seemed that all that boy wanted was the "wild thing". Since I was spayed as a pup, I didn't have any interest in doing the "wild thing". I think that boy was in heat 365 days a year, every time he seen me he would have to stick his nose halfway up my butt. After a while I did get a little snippy with him as I was getting tired of him sniffing me up every time we met. I guess it was my perfume, called "od to old Heidi" that would get him all excited.

Another road trip, how lucky can I get! This time Randy and Kathy were planning a trip down to Arizona to check out the retirement possibilities and see what the heat will be like. I overheard our humans talking about how far they must drive to get to Arizona. Randy keeps thinking it will be over 2,000 miles roundtrip! For my part, the longer the road trip the better. I just love that subtle vibration that the car has it moves down the road, it's so relaxing to sit in the backseat with the air conditioning going and snuggled up close to Jaeger.

The first day was off to a good start. We left Olympia, Washington and didn't make our first stop until we arrived on Oregon. I know that ever few hours I need a drunk of water and a poddy break. I think that silly Jaeger could sleep all day if could get away with it. In northern California we made a stop at a huge olive farm! They didn't seem to have anything that smelled good. Everything seemed to have a vinegar smell to it. Nothing there I wanted to sink my K-9 teeth into. I'm starting to look forward to my suppertime, whenever that may be on this crazy road trip.

We overnighted in central California after briefly visiting a place called Carmel-By-The Sea. A nice scenic town. Randy said he had lived there for nearly two years. He was explaining to Kathy he had lived in his aunt and Uncle's garage until he turned 17 and left to go into the Army. Living in a garage, I hope he had a big kennel to sleep in! I wonder if his food bowl was also in the garage!

The following day we were again traveling down I-5 towards Las Angels. The closed we got to Los Angels the heavier the traffic was. We didn't stop in the city as it seemed intimidating and foreign to Randy and Kathy. We didn't stop for lunch and a poddy stop until we were well outside the city. We stopped just in time because my little doggie legs were crossed, and my bladder was hurting.

Our destination was a Marine base in Arizona that Randy had made reservations for us to spend a few nights and checkout the local offerings. Girlfriend, I thought I was going to melt when I jumped out of the car and onto the pavement. I can immediately see this was not a place fit for this Boxer to live! Jaeger echoed that sediment also. Thank goodness the apartment we were staying in has central air conditioning.

Randy discovered there was a minor problem to solve before we could relax. This military motel requires that Jaeger and I had to be in our kennels during the day when the humans were out and about for the safety of the house keeping staff that came in daily. We don't normally travel with our wire kennels, so now what are we going to do? Randy and Kathy devised a plan to go to the local pet store and buy two collapsible wire kennels. The plan was to assemble them to be used, but the day we start to head home we'll take the kennels back to the pet store and get a refund! Randy and Kathy each took a kennel in and got the refund, problem solved.

Jaeger and I were very relieved when we overheard our humans talking and made the decision that that was not a good retirement area to live. The whole city was packed with retirees everywhere and nothing seemed readily available to rent. We literally just avoided that hot mess! (Pun intended) The drive back wasn't anything significant to mention. Just a lot of airconditioned time riding in the back seat of a giant vibrator with four-wheels and enjoying my personal time with Jaeger. I can't remember ever feeling this blissful.

Chapter four

Let's kick some cancer butt

After we returned to Olympia, I dictated a "Thank You" card that Randy typed up and mailed it to Jaeger. It went like this:

Hello Jaeger,

How is my stud muffin today? This is your cute, brown-eyed Boxer girl over in Tumwater. I wanted to invite you over to my backyard to play. I think there was some mention of BBQ bones. Mumm. Sounds wonderful.

You'll need to ask Kathy to drive you over as she probably will not give you the keys to the car. If out humans weren't so cute, we probably keep them as pets!

Randy can entertain Kathy and I'll
try to keep your "hunky" self-busy. The
Princess awaits.

Heidi Sue

Just as everything was cruising along smoothly,
another crisis arose. My vet found a cancerous mass on
my chest! Oh crap, here we go now. My vet recommended
we see a vet that specializes on treating cancer right here
in Olympia. After seeing the cancer vet and having them
draw fluid off the mass. Unfortunately, the test verified
that it was cancer. Randy seemed so upset with that news!

Fortunately, the cancer vet had offered an idea to trat
my cancer. She recommended a drug that wasn't available
here in the United States yet. Randy got the address from
the vet and sent off for it. Randy said it was a little spendy,
but knew I was worth it. That's another good reason why
I keep this big guy around.

I started that new drug immediately and continued
for three months. Randy was very nice about feeding me
the medication. He used pieces of hot dogs cut into thirds.
Then he would insert the pill into the meat. That was a
win-win situation for everyone. Three months later the
cancer vet said the cancer was gone! What a huge relief

for Randy and myself. I'll miss the daily hot dog that I was taking for the cancer.

Then the unexpected happened. Kathy came over to our place to share with us that Jaeger had passed over into that place she called the "rainbow bridge", she said he had been fighting cancer for a long time. Randy told me that I wouldn't get to see Jaeger anymore which really upset me. That "Rainbow Bridge" thing didn't make any sense to me, (yet.) I'm sure am missing my big fellow's companionship.

About this time Kathy had adopted another Boxer! Her name was Callie, and she was found through a dog rescue organization called "Must Love Boxers". I really enjoyed being around her as she seemed to be a younger version of myself. Callie is so full of energy that I envy!

Unfortunately, she must have found that sugar substitute (xylitol) and ate it. Within a day or two she was gone over the Rainbow Bridge. Callie only lived with Kathy for a few short months before passing on. Kathy was absolutely devastated with losing Callie. I did whatever I could as a Boxer to comfort her. It was so important to try and be some help.

It seems that the years were just flying bye for me. Whenever Randy and Kathy would travel anywhere Jaeger and I would stay at my vacation home, AKA "Top Dog Daycare" in the Olympia, Washington area. I always looked forward to going there. Jaeger and I would share a large kennel. How sweet was that! The boarding was so much fun. The kennel had assigned different playtimes, so I really got a great opportunity to greet and meet other dogs. Most of the dogs are friendly and easy to get along with. I've noticed that my playing has been slowing down a lot lately. With all this white fur on my muzzle I guess I'll have to take ownership for becoming a senior dog.

I think that age is mostly a state of mind. I just keep putting one paw in front of the other. So many dogs to play with and so little time.

Today it's a hot summer day in July and Randy is just wrapping up his garage sale this afternoon. Kathy and Jaeger were here to help with garage sale for a few hours. It just seemed so hot, at times, it was feeling like I couldn't quite catch my breath outside in the driveway. Then suddenly everything went black on me and fell on the asphalt. I can vaguely remember Randy saying something to me, but everything was fading away from me.

Everything is now starting to come back into focus for me. Such bright vivid colors and wonderful smells was so refreshing. No more aches and pains in my body, I almost felt like a young puppy again. OMG, I believe I believe that is the Rainbow Bridge right in front on me. I've heard of rumors about this place, and now I can believe this place really exist.

Chapter Five

The Rainbow Bridge

It's my first day here at the Rainbow Bridge and let me tell you it's been one heck of an adventure! Now I am understanding what I've heard about this place called the "Rainbow Bridge." I could have figured that this place was so wonderful. From the time my paws touched this heavenly ground I was greeted by a joyful park of my furry friends I hadn't seen in years.

First in line to greet me was Jaeger, still the wise and gentle Boxer that he was, he always had a wag and smile for everyone. He gave me a playful nudge and welcomed me with a hearty bark. "Well, well, look at whose finally made it", You're in for a wagging good time here my friend".

Right beside Jaeger was a mischiefs Max. A cheeky Beagle who knows all the best spots for treats. He wagged his tail and said, "Hey there newcomer, brace yourself for more endless games of hide and seek. I've mastered the art of finding all the best treat stashes around here."

As I wagged my tail in excitement I noticed my old buddy, Bella. She was a graceful greyhound known for her lighting fast speed. She gracefully trotted over and gave a gentle nudge. "Welcome to paradise my friend, she whispered, we've got endless open fields here where we can run as fast as the wind."

But the real party started when the mischiefs duo of Milo and Luna arrived. They were a pair of wild and crazy Jack Russell Terriers known for their high energy and antics. Milo did a couple of back flips and Luna twirled in circles before pouncing on me. With wagging tails and puppy kisses. "Woo, a new play buddy in town" they yelped together. We will show the wildest squirrel chasing adventures you've ever seen."

The laughter, the barks, and the wagging tails filled the air as more and more of my old buddies showed up. The playground was buzzing with joy and excitement as if every dog had a supply of trats hidden away.

Amid the happy chaos I couldn't help feeling a sense of belonging and warmth. Each dog their had they're own personality, but we were all unified by our love for life and unwavering loyalty to our human companions. As the sun dropped below the horizon, casting a warm golden glow over the Rainbow Bridge, I couldn't help but to reflect for a few moments had found my place among these incredible souls, and I knew that together we would embark on the most epic and adventures this heavenly realm had to offer.

So, I'm here and I'm living it up at this place called the "Rainbow Bridge". I'm surrounded by my quick witted, funny, smart amid loyal friends who bring out the best in each other. As the night sky twinkles with the brightest stars, we raise our paws and bark in unison, "to friendship, love and the everlasting bonds we share.

I believe that I should continue to enlighten the world to the many secrets that we Boxers hold special. Perhaps some information you will read from my many posts from the Rainbow Bridge and say, "I knew that all along", and for other humans to say, "damn, I didn't know that!" You humans need to stay tuned now there is more wisdom to come your way."

Stanley's Story

Today I have quite a story to share with you, you see, my old pal Stanley had arrived at the Rainbow Bridge not long ago. Stanley and I go way back together. We used to spend our days together, sniffing butts and exploring the neighborhood, causing all kinds of mischief. So, when I heard that Stanley was on his way, I could hardly contain my excitement.

As Stanley approached the Rainbow Bridge, I positioned myself right in the middle, ready to give him a grand welcome. With my paws on my hips and a mischievous grin on my face I barked "Stanley my old buddy "welcome to the Rainbow Bridge." Prepare yourself for eternal belly rubs and endless treat buffets!"

Just as Stanley started across the bridge something strange happened. He tripped over his own paws and tumbled headfirst into a pile of fluff. I couldn't help but to laugh out loud. My tail was wagging so vigorously that it resembled a helicopter propeller. Stanley the clumsy one hadn't changed a bit.

As he dusted himself off, Stanley looked up with a familiar twinkle in his eyes. "Heidi, you old rascal, fancy meeting you here". His voice was filled with both surprise and delight.

We spent hours reminiscing about our days of sneaking into garbage cans, digging holes into the backyard, and then to pretend it wasn't us digging. Oh, the trouble we caused! We laughed so hard our paws hurt and our tails wagged so furiously that they created a gust of wind that sent a squirrel soaring through the sky.

But despite the laughter, a bittersweet realization struck me. I knew that Stanley's arrival meant saying goodbye to our friends on earth, their absence weighed heavy on my heart. I couldn't help but to feel a tingle of sadness.

With a somber wag of my tail, I turned to Stanley and said "you know old friend, as much as I miss our days of chasing mailmen and stealing socks, that there is something truly about this place. It's a haven where all dogs reunite, where we can run freely without leashes and bask in eternal sunshine,"

Stanley nodded in agreement, his eyes filled with a mix of joy and longing. "You're right Heidi, while we've left our earthly companions behind us, we'll hold them in our hearts. Who knows that maybe they'll join us on this glorious adventure."

There we stood, side-by-side gazing out at the vibrant landscape of the Rainbow Bridge. In that moment the air was filled with a sense of hope. A hope the one day we'll be reunited with the humans we loved, chasing squirrels and causing mischief together once more.

So, my dear, though I may be far away, know that I'm sending you an abundance of slobbery kisses and wagging tails from the Rainbow Bridge. Embrace life's adventures, cherish the memories and remember that love knows no boundaries.

Heidi the Pirate

Heidi is known for her witty charm and outlandish antics found herself at the Rainbow Bridge ready to embark on a new adventure. Instead of just frolicking on fluffy clouds, she had a different idea in mind: becoming the most notorious pirate to ever sail the skies.

With a twinkle in her eye and a mischievous grin, Heidi donned a pirate hat, complete with a magical scarf and a tiny eye patch that dangled over her left eye. She fashioned a makeshift pirate ship out of a fluffy cloud and set sail on vast expanse of the Rainbow Bridge.

"Arr me hearties" Heidi bellowed, her tail wagging like a flag in the wind. We be exploring these here skies in search of treasures untold! "Ready your bones boys brace yourselves for this adventure".

Her loyal cloud crew, consisting of playful kittens and playful squirrels scurried about the deck, Raising the fluffy sails and adjusting the cotton ropes. Heidi stood at the helm; paws planted firmly as they set sail to unknown lands.

"Avast ye scurvy scoundrels"" Heidi declared as she pointed a paw upwards towards a particular vibrant rainbow in the distance. "Thar be treasure awaiting us at the end of yonder rainbow! Full speed ahead".

With great gusto the pirate Boxer steered the cloud ship, the wind whipping through her floppy ears. Her crew of fluffy misfits cheered their whiskers were twitching with excitement. The journey fraught with great peril, or so Heidi imagined as she barked orders and navigated through fluffy white cumulus clouds.

As they neared the end of the rainbow Heidi's eyes widened in awe. There nestled among the wisps of colorful light was a chest overflowing with golden dog biscuits and shimmering chew toys.

"Shiver me timbers!" Heidi exclaimed, her pirate heart racing, "we've struck gold me hearties!" Heidi and her crew floated towards the treasure, but just as they reached out to grab their prize, the chest vanished into thin air. The mischievous nature of the Rainbow Bridge outsmarting the most cunning pirates.

"Blimpy!" Heide said as she chuckled and scratched her head. "Seems the magical powers of this here bridge. "Fear not me crew", we may not have treasures in our paws, but we have each other".

With that thought Heidi and her merry band of pirates set sail once more. Exploring the skies with laughter echoing through the air. They discovered fluffy islands inhabited by whimsical animals and shared countless tales of daring escapades.

The pirate Boxer known far and wide as Captain Heidi was not deterred by the elusive treasure, instead she relished in the camaraderie and the joy of the journey, for in this realm of limitless imagination the real treasure lay in the bond's forger with friends and endless laughter that filled the air.

With her pirate's hat tilted rakishly and her tail held high, Captain Heidi sailed the skies of the Rainbow Bridge. Bring laughter and a touch canine mischief to all that crossed her path. For in her heart, she knew that true adventure could not be found in the pursuit of material wealth, but in the joy of embracing life with boundless enthusiasm and a hint of pirate swagger!

The Eyes Have it!

Let's talk about those world famous "puppy eyes"! I know that you humans swoon to those big puppy eyes that us canines master so effortlessly. Ah, that look that melts hearts and tugs at your emotions. Let me give you some insight into this powerful that we Boxers possess.

Yor see my dear friends the sad puppy dog eyes are not just a random facial expression. They are a carefully honed passed down through generations of dogs. They are designed to evolve sympathy, love, and of course treats. We have perfected this look to make you humans unable to resist our charms.

When we gaze at you with those big soulful eyes, it's not because we are unhappy or sad. No, it's our way of communicating. Connecting, and yes, sometimes manipulating. We understand the power of expressions and we use them to our advantage.

Our eyes widen, our brows furrow and we might even let out a little whimper to seal the deal. It's much like an emotional symphony designed to play on your heartstrings. We know that you humans have a soft spot for vulnerability, and we tap into that with our innocent gaze.

Fear not my human friends! We don't use our sad puppy dog eyes for devious purposes alone. We also deploy them to convey genuine emotions. When we're feeling a bit down, when we need comfort and reassurance. Those eyes become a window into our souls. We're asking for a little love and attention, a gentle pat on the head or a cuddle to make everything better.

Let me share another secret with you, we're between our species, a silent understanding not the only ones who benefit from this exchange. You human also experience a profound dense of warmth and affection when you receive that sad puppy look. It's like a magical connection that transcends words.

To appreciate the dept of emotion behind them Feel my unconditional love. Cherish the love and trust that we offer. Also remember it's not just a manipulative ploy for treats. It's a genuine expression of our canine hearts. Let them remind you of the extraordinary bond between humans and dogs.

Embrace the power of those eyes. If you find your heart melting, don't worry you're not alone. It is a universal experience woven into the shared fabric of our shared existence.

Now with this bit of insight dispensed, I'm going to find that area up here that has endless treats. This kind of work builds up my appetite!

The Secret of Zommies

"Attention now you humoons!" Heidi here with more secrets to reveal about the many wonderful Boxer traits we possess.

Prepare yourself for what could possibly one of the most closely guarded Boxer secrets of all times. I know you have often wondered why Boxers dogs go absolutely bonkers and unleash the zoomies upon you!

You see it all starts with our extraordinary ability to tap into the mystical energy of the "silly switch". Yes, you heard it right, the silly switch. Legend has it that buried deep in every Boxer's heart there lies a tiny mischievous fairy called the Zoom Princess Sprinkle Pop. This is where this mischievous little fairy sprinkles its magic dust on us, and the zoomies are unleashed.

But why you may ask do we possess such a phenomenon? Well, it's all part of our mission to keep the world entertained with our hilarious antics. You see, the Zoom Princess Sprinkle Pop being mischievous by nature knows that the world needs a good laugh now and then. So, it activates the silly switch at random moments, turning us Boxers into turbo-charged, whirlwind creatures of pure hilarity.

Imagine this: we start by bouncing around the room like a rubber ball, running into furniture and walls with the grace of a clumsy acrobat. Our faces light up with utter joy and we twist and turn, our tails wagging at supersonic speed. It's as if we were auditioning for the title of "world's most energetic comedian". Providing entertainment for the entire household. We bring smiles, laughter and endless amounts of happiness to those that witness our zoomie extravaganza.

So, the next time you catch a Boxer friend the zoomies, remember its not just an energy burn, but his commitment to bring joy and laughter into your lives,

As we celebrate the absurd phenomenon, lets laugh and cheer the x=zoomies.

Being a Rock Star

Here beyond the Rainbow Bridge is where the bacon is infinite, and the tennis balls never lose their bounce. It has come to my attention that many of you humans are on a quest to find your inner rock star. Well, let me tell you I've been rocking it out up here with my fur=flapping, doing solo and pawsome vocals.!

You see being a Boxer is like being a rock star. We have fans that adore us, we have wild parties. (In the form of fetch sessions). We also have our own version of moves like stage diving when we leap into the air to catch frisbees. The real secret to being a true inner rock star in the proof and wisdom we canines possess. Oh yes, we are more than just another pretty face and wagging tails.

First and foremost, embrace your inner flaws. As a Boxer, I I have a snout that was shorter than some of my canine counterparts. That didn't stop me from rocking it. Absolute not, I used my Unique to sniff out new melodies and unleash my imagination. Don't be afraid to flaunt your inner quirks and imperfections. Turn them into your signature moves, just embrace it!

Now let's talk about fashion. The costumes we dogs can pull off. From being dapper with bow ties to funky bandanas. We know how to make a fashion statement. Embrace your wild side and put on those leather pants and that sparkly jacket. Remember its all about channeling your Mick Jagger,

Lastly and most important. Never forget to have fun. Life is too short to be pawsing and pondering. It's okay to sing at the top of your lungs.

Embrace your flaws, live in the moment. Dress to impress and don't forget to have fun along the way. Now go out there and rock the world with your inner superstar.!

Drooling

Okay now, listen up and I can explain why we Boxers seem to slobber so often. Listen closely my hungry friends, because this tale will make your taste buds tingle and your tails wag with anticipation!

You see us Boxer dogs have an insatiable love for food. Its like an eternal flame that burns within us, constantly reminding of the delicious wonders that the world has to offer. When we catch even the slightest whiff or glimpse of something delectable, our drooling superpowers activate!

Picture this: A juicy steak sizzling on the grill or a fresh batch of mouthwatering cookies cooling on the kitchen counter. Can you blame us for salivating at the sight or smell of such divine culinary creations? Its our way of showing just how much we appreciate the magic that happens in the kitchen.

Why do we Boxers drool more than other breeds you ask? Well, it all comes down to our facial structure. Our magnificent jowls and loose lips give us that signature Boxer face, but they also serve as prime drooling apparatuses. As we salivate in anticipation of a delicious meal, the drool collects in our jowls, forming a gooey masterpiece that can even rival even the most skilled sculptor's work.

Let me tell you its not just the sight or smell of food that gets us going, it's the anticipation, the excitement, and the pure joy of the feast that awaits us. Our drooling is a testament to our zest for life and our unbridled enthusiasm for the culinary delights that make our tails wag with delight.

Now don't be alarmed by our drooling tendencies. It's perfectly normal for us Boxer dogs, an simplify a part of who we are in fact, our drooling can be entertaining! You might catch us with a long stringy trail of drool hanging from out lips, like a canine Picasso painting in progress.

The next time you see a Boxer dog drooling at the sight or smelling food, embrace the moment. It's a testament to out unyielding passion for everything delicious.

Do I smell bacon?

On this day Heidi found herself in a paradise beyond her wildest dreams. As she frolicked through the meadows her nose caught the familiar and tantalizing scent that made her tail wag with uncontrollable excitement, it was the aroma of bacon!

With each step she took the scent grew stronger until Heidi stumbled upon a clearing filled with a magical sight, there, as far as her eyes could see were endless piles of sizzling bacon and stacks of chewy bones. It was a canine heaven made entirely of his favorite treats.

Heidi's eyes widened with delight; she couldn't believe her good luck. She couldn't resist diving in headfirst into the nearest pile of bacon indulging herself in its crispy goodness. With each mouthwatering bite her taste buds danced in pure bliss.

What made this place extraordinary was the fact that Heidi could eat as much as she wanted without ever getting sick or gain an ounce! It was truly the great pleasures of bacon and bones that were endless and guilt free.

As Heidi feasted to her heart's content, she couldn't help to not reflect on the incredible joy that filled the

Rainbow Bridge. It was a place where all dogs could roam free, without pain or worries and indulge in their favorite delights without any limits.

Between mouthfuls of bacon Heidi explored the surrounding landscape. She discovered meandering rivers filled with pure water. Perfect for a refreshing swim after a bacon feast. Lush green fields provided ample space to play fetch and chase imaginary squirrels. The sun always shined brightly casting a warm and very comfortable glow over the entire Rainbow Bridge.

The greatest pleasure for Heidi was not just the abundance of treats and toys, but the comfort of her fellow furry friends. Everywhere she turned she found dogs of every breed, size and color. They were all sharing in the joy and freedom of this wonderous place.

They chased each other's tails and swapped stories of their time on earth and barked with laughter until their sides hurt. It was a community of love and friendship where every wagging tail and wet nose brought comfort and companionship.

As the sun was being to set on the Rainbow Bridge, casting vibrant hues of color across the sky. Heidi took a moment to reflect on her incredible fortune here in the bacon filled paradise she had found a place where happiness knows no bounds.

With a contented sigh, Heidi curled up on a soft cloud. Here belly was full of bacon and a heart filled with gratitude. As she drifted off to sleep, she knew that she would awaken to another glorious day of bacon feasts, endless play and endless joy where every dog's dream comes true.

In this extraordinary real of endless treats and eternal happiness Heidi had found her home. Forever grateful for the blessings of the Rainbow Bridge.

Belly Rubs for Dogs

Hey there my pawsome friends! Today I'm going to explain why belly rubs are so important to us dogs. Let these words fill your heart with joy and a deeper understanding of your furry friends. Whether you are a dog or a human that likes dogs this information can be very helpful in having a deeper understanding of why belly rubs are so important.

You as dogs are positively amazing creatures. You have incredible talents and qualities that make you special. Embrace who you are and show your awesomeness with the world. Keep chasing those dreams! Just like I chase squirrels. You should never give up on the things you truly desire. No bone to big to fetch and no goal is to far to reach.

Every day is a new chance to wag your tail. No matter what happened yesterday, remember that each sunrise brings new opportunities. Embrace the day with a wagging tail and a smile on your face.

Believe in yourself like I believe in you. You are capable of amazing things. Trust your instinct, listen to your heart and have faith in your abilities, you got this.

Embrace the power of pawsitivity! Much in the same as I can turn a sock into an adventure. You can turn any situation into a positive one. Keep that tail wagging and spread good vibes wherever you go.

Remember to play fetch and have fun! Life is to short forget about the simple joys. Take time out to have fun. Life is to short to forget about the simple joys. Take as much time as you can to have fun, play and savior every moment. Play fetch with life and it will always bring you happiness.

Your life is like belly rubs, it makes everything better. Spread love and happiness, much like a good belly rub your love has the power to brighten someone's day and make the world a better place.

Don't be afraid to bark ideas. Your voice matters so be heard. Speak up and share your thoughts and bark your ideas into world. You never know who you might inspire or how you might make a difference. Keep wagging your tail trough challenges. Life can throw you some curve balls but remember to keep that tail wagging, stay resilient, face challenges head on and never forget that you are stronger than you think.

You are loved unconditionally! Just like the way I love my human. Knowing that you are being loved and cherished just the way you are. You are surrounded by a pack of love and support, so never forget that you are never alone.

There you have it! I hope you can find strength and encouragement in these words. Remember to smile and fill your heart with warmth as you are pawsitivity awesome and capable of great things. Keep wagging your tail and embrace life with a dog like enthusiasm.

A good belly rub can cure many things!

Heidi talks about love

This is Heidi coming to you from the Rainbow Bridge with some much-needed insight into the subject of love that applies to dogs and their humans.

Love my dear friends is a wagging tail, a wet nose and a big slobbery kiss. Love is the warmth of a snuggle, the joy of a game of fetch and the trust that never wavers. Love is what makes out tails wag a little faster and our hearts beat a little louder.

Let meg the beauty in each other tell you a secret, love isn't just about romantic gestures or fancy treats. No, love is much more than that. Live is the simple embracing our indifferences and celebrating our unique quirks. It's about seeing the beauty in each other, even if we're a little rough around the edges.

Love is found in the laughter we share; in the games we play, and, in the adventures, we embark upon together. It's the moments of silence when we just understand each or without saying a word. Love is being our true authentic selves, accepting and loving each other exactly the way we are.

Whether you're a dog, human, let's spread love like a wagging tail. Let's shower our loved ones with kisses. Cuddles and kindness. Let's chase after the things that make our heart skip a beat and hold on tightly to the moments that make us feel alive.

Remember that love isn't limited to just one day. Let us make every day a celebration of love, where we wag our tails, laugh out loud and embrace each other with open hearts. Love is what makes the world a little brighter and a whole lot more beautiful. Love fiercely, love unconditionally and love with all your heart.

Ever Lasting Happiness

Here in the whimsical realm of the Rainbow Bridge, Heidi found herself pondering the ever-elusive concept of happiness. With her keen intellect and playful spirit intact. Heidi couldn't help but mull over the intricacies of what it truly meant to be happy.

As she surveyed the joyful scenes of dogs frolicking and humans finding solace in their beloved companions on earth. Heidi scratched her chin and let out a thoughtful "Ruff, ruff". It was time to embark on a quest, a quest for the secrets of everlasting happiness.

With a twinkle in her eye and her tail held high Heidi began her exploration, seeking wisdom from the wise souls who had traversed this eternal place before him. Her first encounter was with an old grey-bearded Saint Bernard named Winston who had an air of serenity about him.

"Winston, my friend" Heidi barked. "What's the secret to happiness"? Winston pondered the answer as he tried to be thoughtful with his answer. "Happiness is much like playing fetch, its not about catching the ball, it's about the joy of chasing it, savior the journey young lady, and let happiness find you along the way". Heidi pondered those words of wisdom as she ventured further, she stumbled upon a mischievous Poodle named Penelope who was known for her knack for getting into mischief.

"Penelope my dear, what is your take on happiness?" Heidi inquired, wagging her tail in anticipation. Penelope grinned mischievously and replied, "Heidi I believe happiness is like a well-executed prank, it catches you off guard and makes you burst into laughter, embrace the unexpected and find joy in life's playful surprises". Amused by Penelope's answer Heidi continued her quest.

Meeting a wise and contemplative Border Collie named Einstein. "Einstein, the master of intelligence, Heidi barked, tell me what's the secret to happiness?" Einstein tilted his head, his wise eyes gleaming, Ah Heidi, happiness is like solving a complex puzzle. It's about using your mind, discovering new perspectives, and never shying away from a challenge. Engage your intellect my friend find happiness in the pursuit of knowledge and growth.".

Heidi nodded appreciatively, absorbing the wisdom bestowed upon her. She realized that happiness was not a destination, but a tapestry of experiences woven together. A harmonious blend of joy, laughter, surprises, and intellectual stimulation.

As Heidi continued her exploration, she encountered an enchanting Labrador named Luna, known for her infectious enthusiasm. "Luna, the bringer of energy and joy!". Heidi exclaimed, "what say you about happiness?" Luna wagged her tail furiously, her eyes sparkling with enthusiasm. "Embrace life's simple pleasures. Happiness is like casing your own tail. It may seem silly and elusive, but the sheer exhilaration of the chase fills your heart with pure delight. Let the happiness within you radiate to the world".

With each encounter Heidi's understanding of happiness deepened. She realized that happiness was not a destination to be reached, but a state of being. A beautiful dance between the heart, mind and soul.

Returning to her spot on the Rainbow Bridge, Heidi sat with her newfound wisdom and a rather mischievous twinkle in her eye. She believes that she has found an understanding of happiness. So with a wag of her tail and a joyful bark, Heidi resolved to spread happiness from the Rainbow Bridge. She sent playful gust of wind to make children giggle, whispered comforting words the ears of the lonely and showered extra love on those in need of a canine companion.

For Heidi knew that true happiness lay not in possession or achievement, but in the act of spreading joy to others.

As she watched the smiles light up the faces of humans and dogs alike. Heidi could help to not think. "Perhaps happiness is not a puzzle to be solved, but a gift to be shared".

From that day forward Heidi the Boxer became the jester of the Rainbow Bridge, spreading laughter, love and happiness to all who crossed her path. For in the realm of eternal joy, Heidi had discovered the essence of happiness. To just simplify brighten the lives of others an in turn find boundless happiness within herself.

This now ends the communication with Heidi at the Rainbow Bridge as she now proceeds with her quest to create and spread happiness.

Printed in the United States
by Baker & Taylor Publisher Services